For Tom and Freya with all my love, with special thanks to Leo and Humphrey for good advice and most of all to Noah for the inspiration

First American Edition 2017
Kane Miller, A Division of EDC Publishing

Copyright © 2017 Jane Porter

Published by arrangement with Walker Books Ltd, 87 Vauxhall Walk, London SE11 5HJ

For information contact:
Kane Miller, A Division of EDC Publishing
PO Box 470663
Tulsa, OK 74147-0663
www.kanemiller.com
www.edcpub.com
www.usbornebooksandmore.com

Library of Congress Control Number: 2016955631

Printed in China
1 2 3 4 5 6 7 8 9 10

ISBN: 978-1-61067-611-3

PINK LION

Jane Porter

Kane Miller

A DIVISION OF EDC PUBLISHING

Arnold's life
was just right.

His family loved him.

They ate the nicest food.
And every day they
played games down
at the water hole.

One day, a growling gang bounced by.

"It's a PINK lion!" they said.

"Living with a lot of BIRDS!"

"What's he doing here? He's supposed to be part of OUR family."

"I'm a lion?" asked Arnold, puzzled.
"Yes, look at your face in the water,"
said one of the lions.

It was true, they did look alike.
They had the same curly hair and whiskers.
Could they really be related?
"Come along with us," said the
lions. "You should be out
roaring and hunting!"

Arnold thought perhaps he should give it a try.
"This is how we hunt," said the lions,
and off they raced.

Arnold wasn't sure he could run that fast.

"Next, some washing," said the lions.
"It's easy – just stick out your tongue
and lick!"

Arnold wasn't used to the furry taste, and wished he had his soap and sponge. Being a lion was very different from life at home.

RRRROOOOOOOOOAR!

Squork

"Squork," said Arnold.

"I'm sorry," he said. "You've been very kind, but I just can't do it. I'm not a proper lion. I think I'll go back to my family now."

But when he got home, something terrible had happened. A very nasty crocodile had moved in.

"Excuse me," said Arnold, "this is our water hole."

"Not anymore," said the crocodile. "It's time you and your feathery friends moved on. I live here now."

Arnold didn't know what to say.

He looked at the sky.

He looked at the ground.

And then a strange feeling
like a hairy ball rose up
from deep inside
him ...

... and burst out of his mouth with a mighty

The other lions heard Arnold calling.
Together they chased that crocodile
until he wished he had never
seen the water hole.

ROOOOAR!

And Arnold's roar
was the **loudest** and
fiercest of all.

After that, life for Arnold went back to being just right again. And bath time with his new cousins was more fun than ever.